IN SEARCH OF THE MASK

The Sons of Garmadon already collected two powerful Oni Masks.
Now they are looking for the third one, and the ninja need to stop them.
Look at the picture fragments and mark the ones that fit the main image.

LET'S FIND THE MASK OF HATRED! USE THE CODE ON THE NEXT PAGE TO COLOR IT IN SO WE'LL RECOGNIZE IT WHEN WE SEE IT.

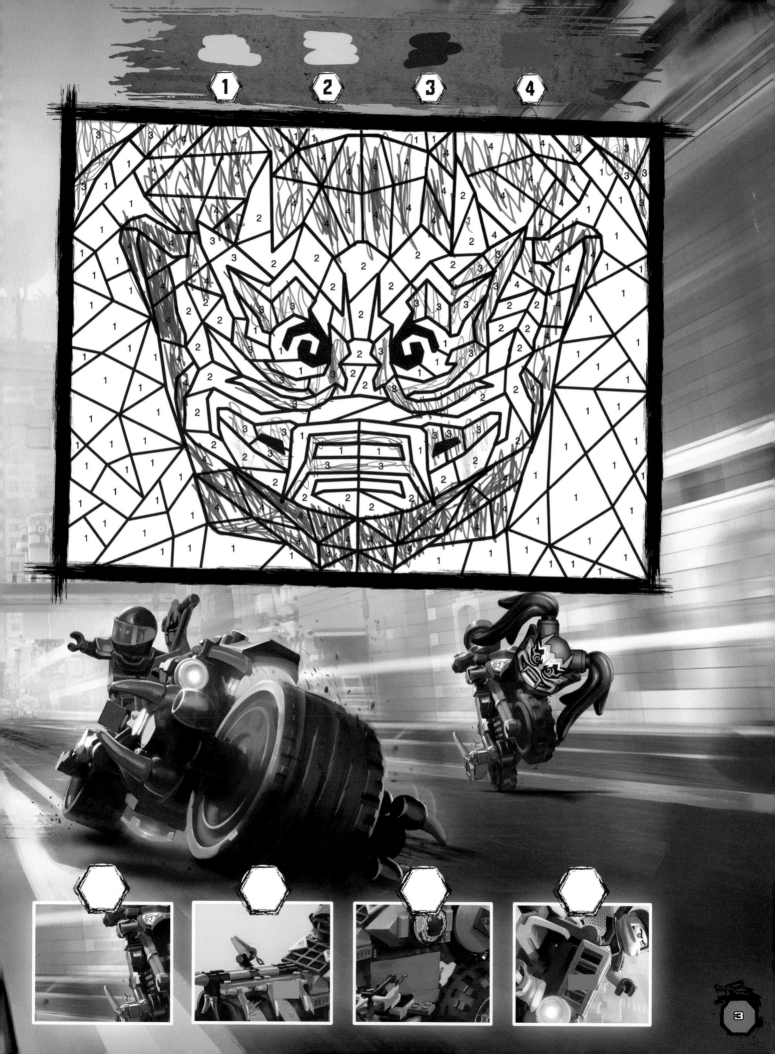

ACROSS THE SWAMP

Lloyd and Harumi want to find the final Oni Mask before the Sons of Garmadon do. Help them reach it. It's hidden inside the Oni Temple on the other side of a swamp maze.

ROCK TRAP

The final Oni Mask is hidden on the other side of this huge chasm. Follow the arrows to help Lloyd find a safe path to the other side.

TO TAME A GIANT CRAB

ARRRRGH!! THERE'S A GIANT CRAB COMING STRAIGHT FOR US!

I WISH WE HAD SOME FOOD. THEN WE COULD TAME IT AND RIDE IT BACK TO NINJAGO CITY!

HMM . . . I'VE GOT SOME BUBBLE GUM IN MY POCKET!

EWWWWW!

THROW IT AT THE CRAB, QUICK!

I THINK I HAVE HALF A PANCAKE IN MY BACKPACK!

IT WAS SUPER TASTY THREE DAYS AGO.

OOPS . . . RUN!

LOOK! I HAVE BROCCOLI IN MY BAG.

DO CRABS LIKE VEGETABLES?

YEAH — I DIDN'T THINK SO.

WHAT ABOUT YOU, ZANE?

I HAVE A BOX OF FISH FINGERS IN MY KNAPSACK.

LOOK AT CRABBY GO! HE LOVES THEM!

ZANE, YOU'RE A NINDROID. YOU DON'T EAT. SO HOW COME YOU HAD A BOX OF FROZEN FISH FINGERS?

IT'S PERFECTLY LOGICAL . . . BUT FIRST, YOU BETTER EXPLAIN WHY YOU HAD A PANCAKE IN YOUR BACKPACK FOR THREE DAYS!

TEMPLE FIGHT

Harumi has trapped Lloyd . . . and revealed that she's the leader of the Sons of Garmadon! Fortunately, the other ninja have come to his rescue. Look at the pictures from before and after Lloyd's rescue. Then mark the parts of the temple that were damaged.

Harumi is in jail, but she still managed to bring back Lo...
now he's more evil than ever! It's up to you to help Lloyd...
Can you find the sword moves he'll need in the boxes belo...
correct answers in the empt...

Lloy
ont
of

ATTACKS:

¥	thrust
ろ	cut from the left
떼	cut from the right
乂	cut from the top

DEFENSE:

against cuts from the top	凹
against cuts from the left	朩
against thrusts	中
against cuts from the right	人

NAWAY TRAIN

d is trying to escape from Harumi! The Green Ninja escaped
o a city tram with little Wu in his arms. Can you help the crew
Destiny's Bounty find them? Circle the correct tram route.

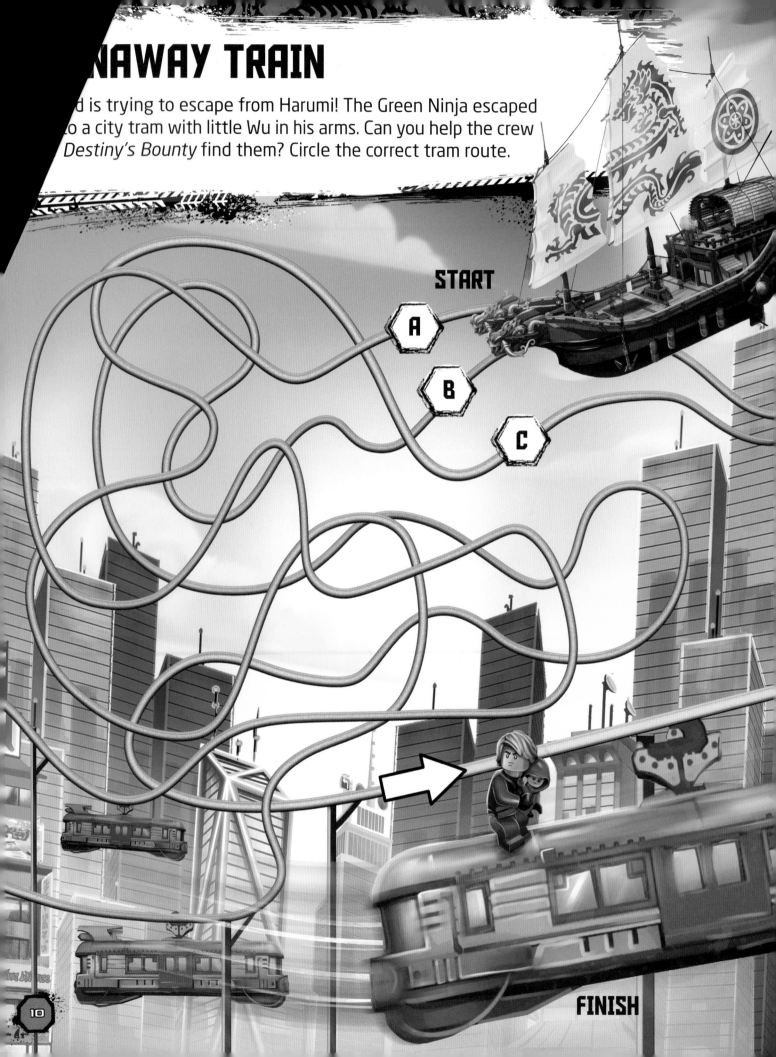

START

A

B

C

FINISH

DESTINY'S FINAL FLIGHT

The Oni Titan grabbed the *Destiny's Bounty* and cracked it into pieces. Which of the fragments below match the ship? Write the correct letters inside the empty spaces.

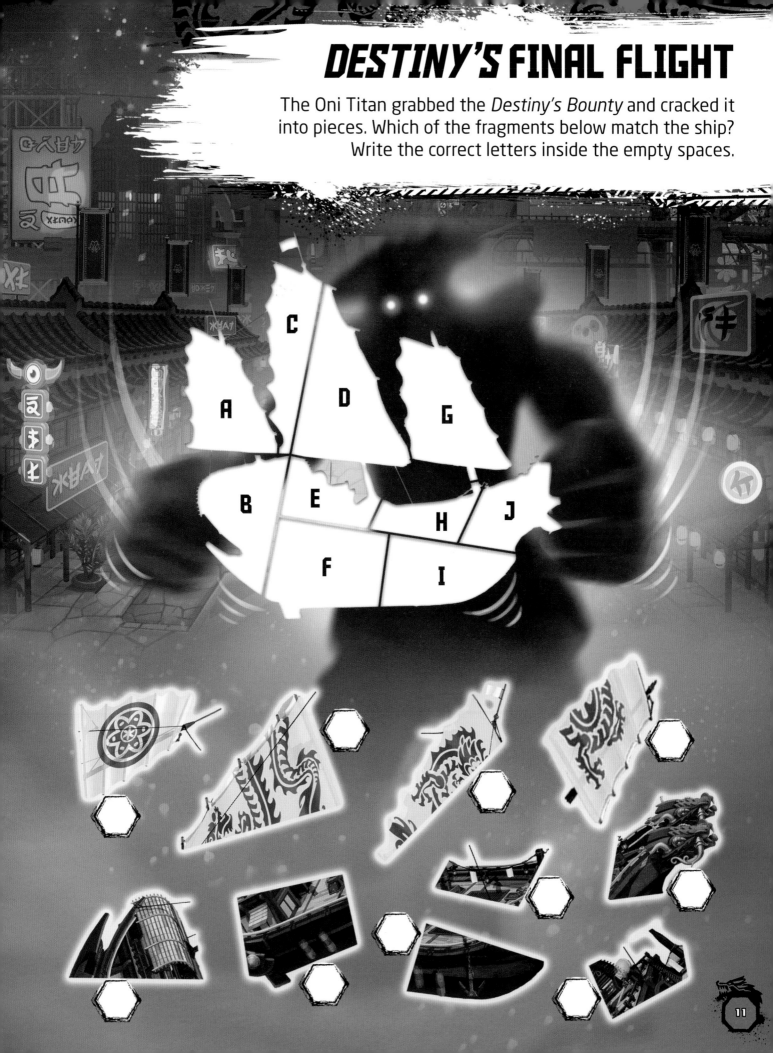

STRANGE LAND

The *Destiny's Bounty* suddenly disappeared from Ninjago City! It has been mysteriously transported into the Realm of Oni and Dragon. But was anyone inside? Look for the ninja's names inside the word bank to find out!

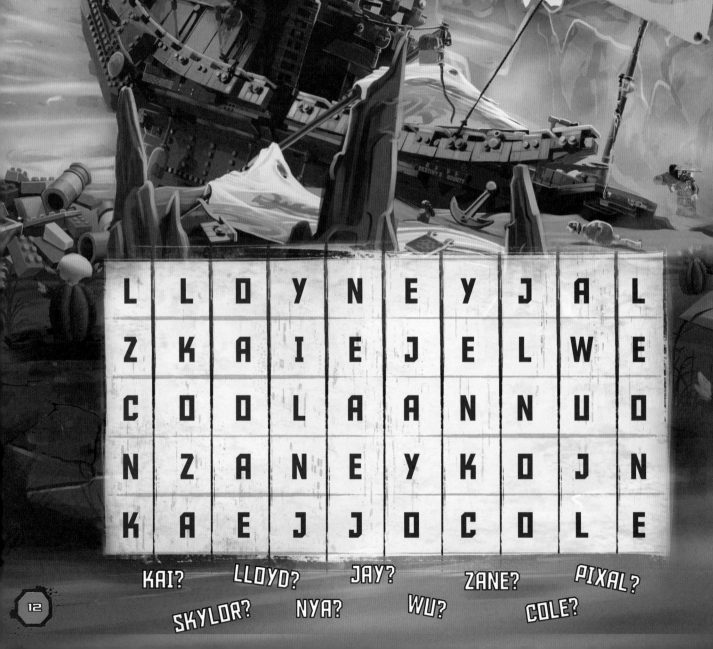

L	L	O	Y	N	E	Y	J	A	L
Z	K	A	I	E	J	E	L	W	E
C	O	O	L	A	A	N	N	U	O
N	Z	A	N	E	Y	K	O	J	N
K	A	E	J	J	O	C	O	L	E

KAI? LLOYD? JAY? ZANE? PIXAL?

SKYLOR? NYA? WU? COLE?

WASTELAND CHASE

The ninja are stranded in an alien realm — and they're on the run again. This time, the fierce Dragon Hunters are on their trail! But Jay managed to find a way through the maze of canyons. Can you show his friends the way he took?

START

FINISH

OUT OF THE FIRE

YOU'RE PRISONERS OF THE DRAGON HUNTERS!

COME ON! WE GATECRASHED THIS PLACE BY ACCIDENT.

HUH? BY ACCIDENT?

YEAH, WE HAD SOME MAGIC TEA AND . . .

. . . YOU KNOW THAT ALWAYS ENDS BADLY.

WE'RE NOT LOOKING FOR TROUBLE.

LOOKS LIKE YOU FOUND SOME ANYWAY.

IT LOOKS LIKE WE HAVE — LOOK OUT!

YOU CAN'T FOOL US THAT EASILY!

WE'RE NOT GOING TO LOOK AWAY WHILE YOU ESCAPE!

FRIENDS TO THE RESCUE!

Oh no! Jay, Kai, and Zane were captured! Cole wants to rescue his friends, but first he needs to figure out when the guards will change their posts, and in what order. Can you help him? Write the correct numbers below, and make sure that no Dragon Hunter appears more than once in each row and column.

DARETH'S DARING ESCAPE

The Sons of Garmadon are trailing Dareth in hopes of he'll lead them to the Resistance headquarters. Can you help the Brown Ninja shake off his enemies? Follow the arrows to reach the meeting place undiscovered.

THE TERRIBLE TITAN

Ninjago City is in a state of terror. The powerful Oni Titan is so strong, no one dares to stand up to it – or to its master, Lord Garmadon. Can you tell which shadow belongs to the stone giant? Circle the two identical shadows among the fake ones.

WANTED: LLOYD GARMADON

The Sons of Garmadon will do everything in their power to capture Lloyd.
Take a look at the wanted posters they've made of the Green Ninja.
Can you find the details that make each one different?
Circle the differences.

BREAK OUT!

BY SUE BEHRENT

Locked inside a dark cell, the ninja whispered to one another.

"We have to escape from the Dragon Hunters today," said Kai, "while Iron Baron and Heavy Metal are away on their scavenging mission."

"But even if we escape, we will still be stuck in the Realm of Oni and Dragon," said Zane.

"True, but anything's better than being trapped here with these jokers," said Jay. "First they steal our gear, then they expect us to repair it for them. I can't take it anymore!"

"Shhhhh!" Kai hissed. "The only chance we have to escape is when they let us outside to work. We all know the plan . . ."

Just then, the cell door creaked open.

"Out, you three!" Daddy-No-Legs ordered. "Get to work!"

* * *

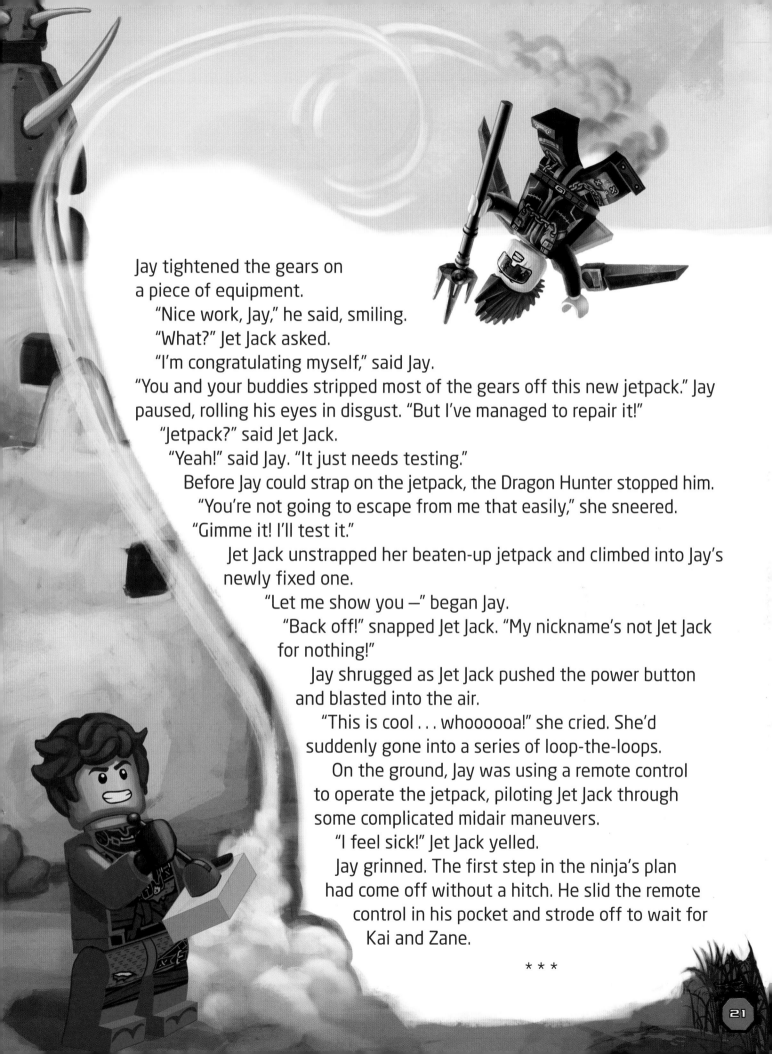

Jay tightened the gears on a piece of equipment.

"Nice work, Jay," he said, smiling.

"What?" Jet Jack asked.

"I'm congratulating myself," said Jay. "You and your buddies stripped most of the gears off this new jetpack." Jay paused, rolling his eyes in disgust. "But I've managed to repair it!"

"Jetpack?" said Jet Jack.

"Yeah!" said Jay. "It just needs testing."

Before Jay could strap on the jetpack, the Dragon Hunter stopped him.

"You're not going to escape from me that easily," she sneered. "Gimme it! I'll test it."

Jet Jack unstrapped her beaten-up jetpack and climbed into Jay's newly fixed one.

"Let me show you —" began Jay.

"Back off!" snapped Jet Jack. "My nickname's not Jet Jack for nothing!"

Jay shrugged as Jet Jack pushed the power button and blasted into the air.

"This is cool . . . whoooooa!" she cried. She'd suddenly gone into a series of loop-the-loops.

On the ground, Jay was using a remote control to operate the jetpack, piloting Jet Jack through some complicated midair maneuvers.

"I feel sick!" Jet Jack yelled.

Jay grinned. The first step in the ninja's plan had come off without a hitch. He slid the remote control in his pocket and strode off to wait for Kai and Zane.

* * *

Meanwhile, across the compound . . .

"SNAP!" Arkade screeched, throwing down a card and slapping his hand on top of the pile.

"You may only call 'snap' if the card you put down matches the card I just put down," Zane grumbled as he pulled Arkade's hand off the cards and scooped them up. "These. Do. Not. Match. Which means I win!"

"No fair," whined Arkade. "You should be working on that motor anyway, not playing games!"

"Fine," said Zane. He calmly put down the deck of cards.

As Zane began working on the motor, Arkade gathered up the pack and began shuffling the cards.

Zane nodded, satisfied. Then he slipped away to meet Jay.

* * *

"You've never had an oil change?" Kai asked Daddy-No-Legs as he poured the *Destiny's Bounty* oil supply into a row of containers. "You must have a lot of sand in your leg gears . . ."

"Iron Baron wouldn't like —" began Daddy-No-Legs.

"... In fact I know you do," continued Kai. "We hear you squeaking around the compound at night."

"You do?!" asked Daddy-No-Legs.

"It keeps us awake!" said Kai.

"I suppose a little squeeze of spare oil might be okay . . ." said Daddy-No-Legs.

"Exactly! I'll put a bit of — uh-oh, I'm sooooooo clumsy!" said Kai, spilling oil over the workbench. "I'll get the mop."

Kai used the mop to spread the oil all over the floor.

"You're making a bigger mess!" screamed Daddy-No-Legs. "Give me that dirty mooooooooop!"

Daddy-No-Legs slipped in the slick puddle of oil, his mechanical legs flailing in all directions.

"ARRRRRRRGH!" he cried as he skidded across the floor. He grabbed Kai's hand to try and steady himself. But instead, the two of them spun around in dizzy circles.

"My hands are too oily!" said Kai. "I'm losing my grip!"

Kai slipped from Daddy-No-Leg's grasp and flew out of the door of the workshop. He landed right at Heavy Metal's feet. Kai let out of a groan of pain . . . which quickly turned into a groan of despair when he saw who stood behind Heavy Metal. It was Jay and Zane . . . and they were back in handcuffs.

* * *

"Fools! The prisoners were trying to distract you so they could escape!" Heavy Metal shouted. He'd already locked the ninja back in their cell. "And if I hadn't returned, they would've gotten away!"

Daddy-No-Legs looked ashamed. Jet Jack was still too dizzy from all the loop-the-loops to speak. Arkade silently fiddled with his playing cards.

"Give me those, Arkade," snarled Heavy Metal. "Now, you three get out of my sight! No more card games for you until you learn how to play to win, like me!"

* * *

Later that evening, Heavy Metal sighed as Iron Baron slammed his claw down on the table between them.

"SNAP!" Iron Baron yelled triumphantly as he threw a two card on top of a ten card.

"Good game, boss," said Heavy Metal wearily. "You win."

HUNTERS' FAVORITE GAME

The Dragon Hunters' love playing card games. Follow the arrows to figure out the order in which the cards are laid out. Then decide which cards go in the empty spaces to complete the pattern.

DON'T LOSE HOPE!

Lloyd and the Resistance have broken into the TV station inside Garmadon's headquarters to send a message of hope to the citizens of Ninjago City. Can you help them connect the main camera to the right plug?

THIS ISN'T THE FIRST TIME OUR CITY HAS FACED DISASTER. BUILDINGS MAY FALL, BUT WE WILL RISE.

FIX DIESELNAUT

Dieselnaut is a beast of a vehicle, but it breaks a lot. That's why the Dragon Hunters need a large supply of spare parts for longer trips. Can you find the parts that fit the machine? Write the correct number next to the part.

EVACUATE THE HQ!

Lloyd, Nya, Dareth, and Skylor barely escaped the S.O.G. attack against the Resistance HQ. Can you lay out an escape plan for them? First use the coordinates to mark the places that have enemy patrols!

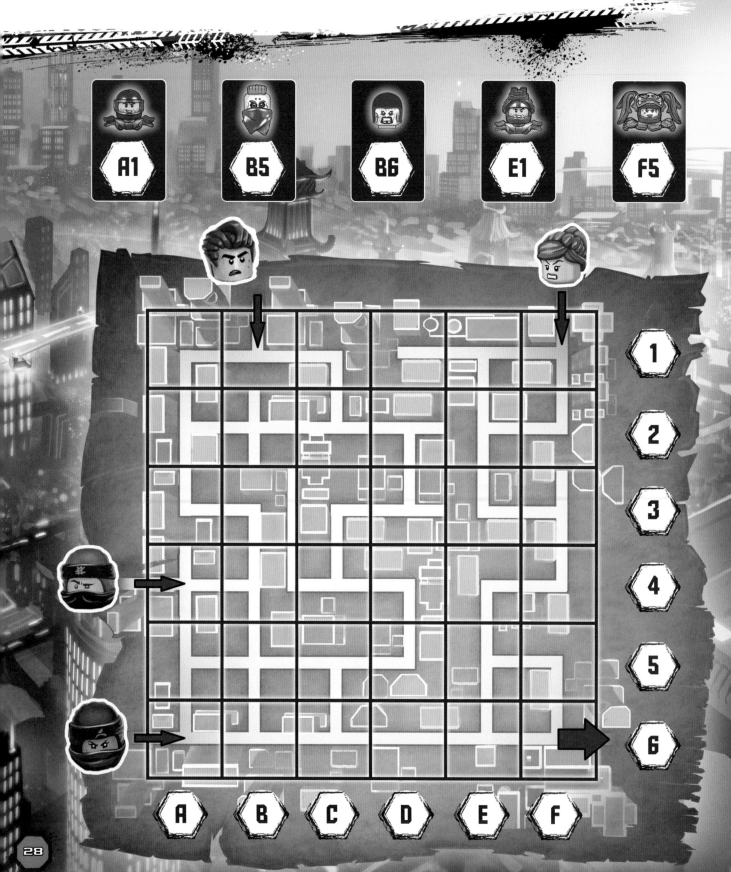

Cole, Kai, Zane, and Jay came up with an idea to escape. They are designing something to distract the guards. Connect the dots in the right order to find out what they came up with.

ANSWERS

pgs. 2-3

pg. 4

pg. 5

pg. 8

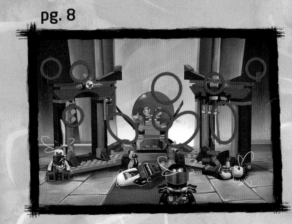

pg. 9

pg. 11

C
D
A
B
G
E
H
J
F
I

pg. 12

L	L	O	Y	N	E	Y	J	A	L
Z	K	A	I	E	J	E	L	W	E
C	O	O	L	A	A	N	N	U	O
N	Z	A	N	E	Y	K	O	J	N
K	A	E	J	J	O	C	O	L	E

pg. 10

Pg. 13

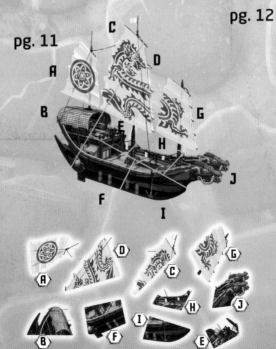

pg. 16

pg. 17

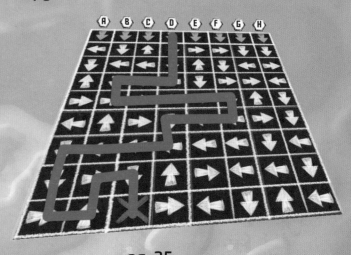

pg. 18

pg. 19

WANTED

WANTED

WANTED

WANTED

pg. 25

pg. 26

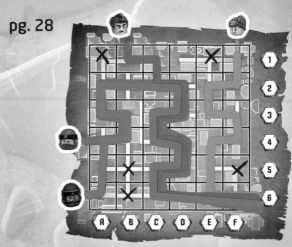

pg. 28

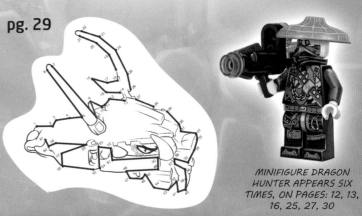

pg. 27

pg. 29

MINIFIGURE DRAGON HUNTER APPEARS SIX TIMES, ON PAGES: 12, 13, 16, 25, 27, 30